Spooked

THE MOST HAUNTED PLACES IN THE WORLD

BY EMILY RAIJ

Reading Consultant:

Barbara J. Fox
Professor Emerita
North Carolina State University

CAPSTONE PRESS
a capstone imprint

Blazers Books are published by Capstone Press,
1710 Roe Crest Drive, North Mankato, Minnesota 56003
www.capstonepub.com

Library of Congress Cataloging-in-Publication Data
Raij, Emily, author.
The most haunted places in the world / by Emily Raij.
    pages cm. — (Blazers books. Spooked!)
Summary: "Describes ten of the most haunted places in the world"— Provided by publisher.
Audience: Ages 8-14
Audience: Grades 4 to 6
ISBN 978-1-4914-4076-6 (library binding)
ISBN 978-1-4914-4110-7 (ebook pdf)
1. Haunted places—Juvenile literature. 2. Ghosts—Juvenile literature. I. Title.
BF1461.R343 2016
133.1'2—dc23
                                        2015001333

Editorial Credits

Anna Butzer, editor; Kyle Grenz, designer; Morgan Walters, media researcher; Kathy McColley, production specialist

Photo Credits

Alamy: The Marsden Archive, 14, 15, toby de silva, 10, 11; Getty Images: PhotoQuest, 18, 19, Syfy, 27; iStockphoto: ImagineGolf, 12, 13, JohnGollop, background 32; Shutterstock: D_D, (vintage photo frames) throughout, Balazs Kovacs Images, 28, 29, D_D, (paper notes) throughout, Dean Fikar, 6, 7, Delmas Lehman, 1, jan kranendonk, cover, kenkistler, cover, littleny, 22, 23, Marek Stefunko, 20, 21, Maria Dryfhout, 4, 5, Nickolay Stanev, 8, 9, Ross Strachan, 16, 17, Sociologas, (old photo strip) throughout, SSokolov, 2, 3, 30, 31, trekandshoot, 24, 25, Tueris, (grunge texture) throughout

Printed in China by Nordica
0415/CA21500562
032015   008844NORDF15

TABLE OF CONTENTS

CREEPY CAUSES

Scraaaaatch! Is that a branch brushing up against the window, or is your house haunted? Some people think ghosts are real. The following places around the world are famous for their haunted happenings.

THE ALAMO

In 1836 a bloody battle took place at the Alamo in San Antonio, Texas. The 13-day battle killed hundreds of people. Today visitors claim to see **spirits** of dead soldiers walking around this famous place.

spirit—the soul or invisible part of a person that is believed to control thoughts and feelings

DID YOU KNOW?

The Alamo was originally built in the 1700s as a place of worship.

ALCATRAZ ISLAND

In 1934 officials opened a prison on Alcatraz
Island in San Francisco, California, for the
toughest **criminals**. Many prisoners died there
before the doors closed in 1963. Guards and
prisoners reported strange sounds, smells, and
sights. Visitors today say Alcatraz is still haunted.

DID YOU KNOW?

The **gangster** Al Capone is the most famous ghost believed to haunt Alcatraz. He played the banjo. Visitors sometimes hear banjo music in the shower room.

criminal—someone who commits a crime

gangster—a member of a criminal gang

AMITYVILLE HOUSE

In 1974 Ronald DeFeo Jr. killed his family in their home in Amityville, New York. George and Kathy Lutz bought the house in 1975. They heard strange noises and felt sudden temperature changes. After 28 days the Lutzes left the house in fear. Was this a **hoax** or a real haunting?

hoax—a trick to make people believe something that is not true

BANFF SPRINGS HOTEL

Banff Springs Hotel in Alberta, Canada, opened in 1888. Several ghosts are said to haunt this hotel. One ghost is a bride who died falling down a staircase. Other guests report seeing ghosts of a murdered family and a dead **bellman** named Sam.

bellman—someone employed to run errands and carry luggage around hotels

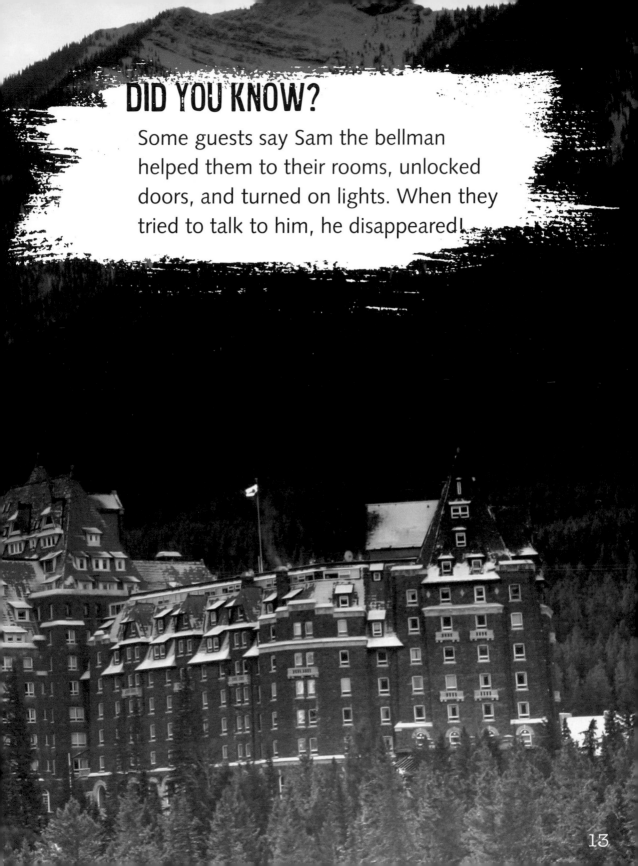

DID YOU KNOW?

Some guests say Sam the bellman helped them to their rooms, unlocked doors, and turned on lights. When they tried to talk to him, he disappeared!

BORLEY RECTORY

The Borley **Rectory** in Essex, England, has been haunted since it was built in 1862. The mansion's residents and visitors reported ghosts, eerie footsteps, and mysterious bones. Stones are thrown when no one is around. The rectory burned down in 1939.

DID YOU KNOW?

Researchers have studied the strange activities at the Borely Rectory. Some of the activities cannot be explained.

rectory—a house or building where church leaders live

researcher—someone who studies a subject to discover new information

15

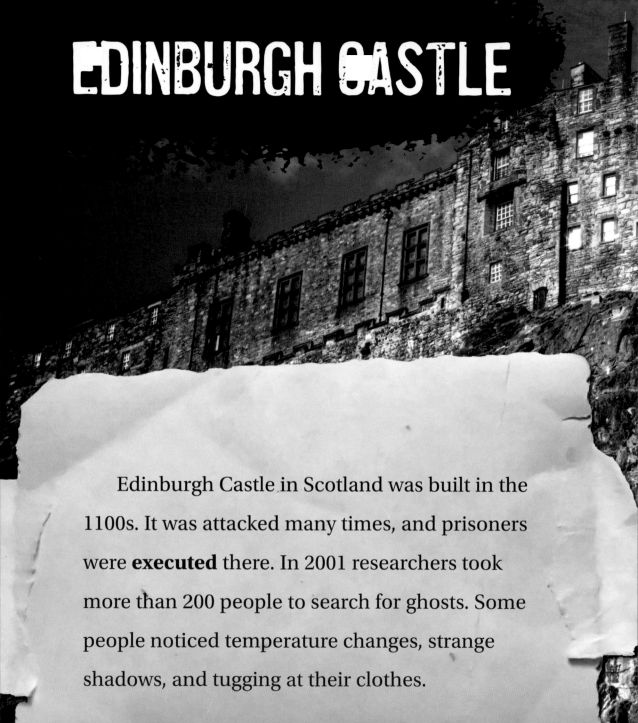

EDINBURGH CASTLE

Edinburgh Castle in Scotland was built in the 1100s. It was attacked many times, and prisoners were **executed** there. In 2001 researchers took more than 200 people to search for ghosts. Some people noticed temperature changes, strange shadows, and tugging at their clothes.

execute—to put to death as punishment for a crime

GETTYSBURG

One of the bloodiest battles of the Civil War (1861–1865) took place at Gettysburg, Pennsylvania, in 1863. Thousands of soldiers were killed in just three days. Today visitors report seeing ghosts of soldiers on the battlefield and guarding Gettysburg College.

THE TOWER OF LONDON

England's Tower of London was built in the 1000s. It was used as a prison and place of execution. King Henry VIII had his wife Anne Boleyn held and killed there in 1536. Today soldiers guarding the tower say they see and feel her spirit rush past them.

DID YOU KNOW?

The Tower of London is not actually a tower. It is an entire castle.

THE QUEEN MARY

The *Queen Mary* is a floating hotel in Long Beach, California. It was used as a warship during World War II (1939–1945). Visitors report seeing sailors' ghosts and hearing the voices of two girls who drowned in the pool. Guests also say spooky things happen in the kitchen where a cook was killed.

DID YOU KNOW?

At the beginning of World War II, the *Queen Mary* was painted gray and given the nickname the "Gray Ghost."

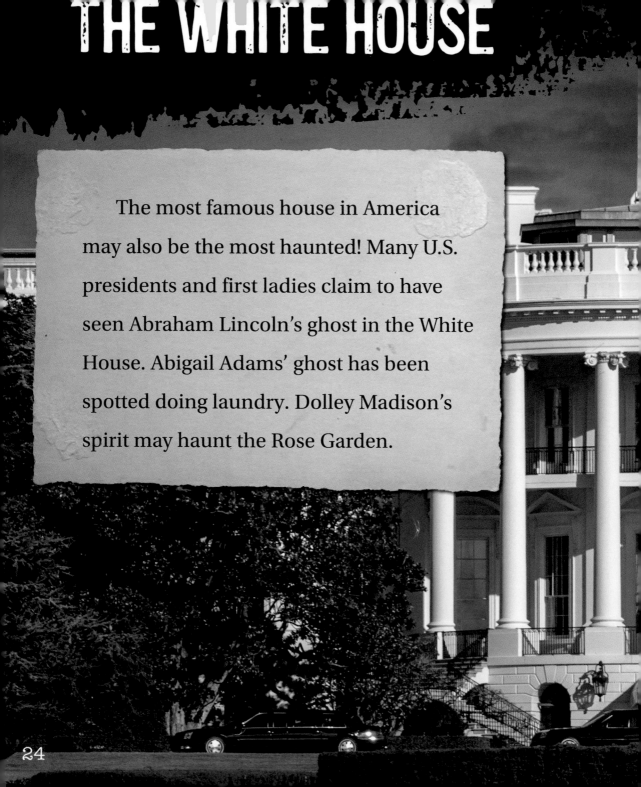

THE WHITE HOUSE

The most famous house in America may also be the most haunted! Many U.S. presidents and first ladies claim to have seen Abraham Lincoln's ghost in the White House. Abigail Adams' ghost has been spotted doing laundry. Dolley Madison's spirit may haunt the Rose Garden.

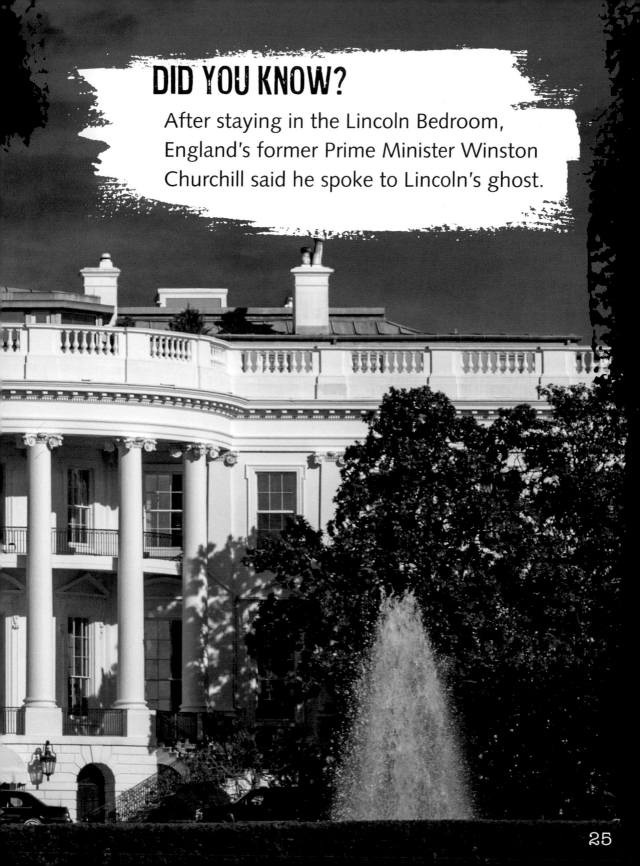

DID YOU KNOW?

After staying in the Lincoln Bedroom, England's former Prime Minister Winston Churchill said he spoke to Lincoln's ghost.

PARANORMAL INVESTIGATORS

Paranormal investigators study haunted houses. They take photos and record strange sounds or temperature changes. Skeptics say there is no proof of hauntings. Natural causes can explain strange sights, sounds, and feelings.

paranormal investigator—someone who studies events that science can't explain

skeptic—a person who questions things that other people believe to be true

proof—facts or evidence that something is true

DID YOU KNOW?

Investigators say the temperature can drop 10 degrees Fahrenheit (5.6 degrees Celsius) when a ghost is in the room.

HAUNTED OR NOT?

There is no way to know for sure if ghosts exist. Some **mysteries** turn out to be hoaxes while others are harder to explain with science. Either way, it's fun to wonder if spooky spirits are real! Maybe someday you'll get to visit a haunted place. Maybe you already have!

mystery—something that is hard to explain or understand

GLOSSARY

bellman (BELL-muhn)—someone employed to run errands and carry luggage around hotels

criminal (KRI-muh-nuhl)—someone who commits a crime

execute (EK-si-kyoot)—to put to death as punishment for a crime

gangster (GANG-stur)—a member of a criminal gang

hoax (HOHKS)—a trick to make people believe something that is not true

mystery (MISS-tur-ee)—something that is hard to explain or understand

paranormal investigator (pa-ruh-NOR-muhl in-VESS-tuh-gate-ur)—someone who studies events that science can't explain

proof (PROOF)—facts or evidence that something is true

rectory (REK-tuh-ree)—a house or building where church leaders live

researcher (REE-surch-ur)—someone who studies a subject to discover new information

skeptic (SKEP-tik)—a person who questions things that other people believe to be true

spirit (SPIHR-it)—the soul or invisible part of a person that is believed to control thoughts and feelings

READ MORE

Chandler, Matt. *The World's Most Haunted Places.* The Ghost Files. Mankato, Minn.: Capstone Press, 2011.

Williams, Dinah. *Dark Mansions.* Scary Places. New York: Bearport Pub. Co., 2012.

Williams, Dinah. *Haunted Prisons.* Scary Places. New York: Bearport Pub. Co., 2014.

INTERNET SITES

FactHound offers a safe, fun way to find Internet sites related to this book. All of the sites on FactHound have been researched by our staff.

Here's all you do:

Visit *www.facthound.com*

Type in this code: 9781491440766

Check out projects, games and lots more at
www.capstonekids.com

INDEX